A · A · Milne

A GALLERY OF CHILDREN

A REPRODUCTION OF THE MILNE CLASSIC

Illustrated by HENRIETTE WILLEBEEK LE MAIR

GALLERY CHILDREN'S BOOKS

LONDON AND THE HAGUE

Illustrations copyright © 1989 by Soefi Stichting Inayat Fundatie Sirdar.
Text reprinted by permission of Harrap
Publishing Group Ltd.
Published by Gallery Children's Books an
Imprint of East-West Publications (UK) Ltd,
Newton Works, 27/29 Macklin Street, London
WC2B 5LX. All inquiries to
East-West Publications.
Printed and bound in Hong Kong by the South
China Printing Company. (1988) Limited
ISBN 0 85692 179 3

Contents

The Princess and the Apple Tree
5

Sparrow Tree Square
11

The Twins
17

Miss Waterlow in Bed
23

Poor Anne
29

A Voyage to India
35

Barbara's Birthday
41

The Magic Hill
47

The Baby Show
53

The Three Daughters of M. Dupont
59

Castles by the Sea
65

A Note About the Book
72

The Princess and the Apple Tree

*"Come, it's time for a story," called the oldest
sister as the rain fell outside.
And so the five sisters sat under their
favorite umbrella tree, perfect for listening
to stories, as their oldest sister began . . .*

ONCE upon a time there was a beautiful princess, who loved all lovely things, and most she loved the flowers and the blossoming trees in her father's garden. Now there was a humble man called Silvio, whose business it was to tend the flowers and the trees in the King's garden, and to him also they were a never-ending happiness, because of their beauty. So it was that their love for lovely things drew them together, and Silvio loved the Princess, and sometimes they walked hand in hand together.

But the King was angry, for it was in his mind that the Princess should marry a greater man than this; and he came upon Silvio in the garden and commanded him to leave that country and never to be found there again. And Silvio said, "How can I leave the garden which I love?" Whereupon the King laughed, and said, "Stay, then," and touched him with the wand which he carried . . . and in a moment there was no Silvio there, but only another apple tree in the garden. For the King of that country was a great magician, and many were afraid of him.

The days went by, and still the Princess sought Silvio in the garden, but he did not come. So she went to her father, the King, and asked of him. And the King laughed, and said, "He was pruning an apple tree. I did not like the way he pruned it. He will never come back." Then the Princess said, "Which was the tree he was pruning?" And the King led her to the window and showed her the tree. And the Princess was astonished, for she did not know that there had been an apple tree there. And, when she was alone, she went to the apple tree, saying, "It is the last thing which he touched"; so she touched it with her hand. And the apple tree trembled gently, and the blossom fell upon her head. So it was on the next day, and the next . . .

And summer came, but Silvio did not come, and autumn came, and still she thought of Silvio. One day, while she was beneath the apple tree, she cried out suddenly, "O Silvio, let me not forget you!" — and the tree shook, and an apple fell into her lap. The Princess took a little silver knife and peeled the apple, so that the peel was unbroken, and she threw the peel over her shoulder, saying, "See whom I

love!" And she looked behind her, and there was the letter *S* upon the ground. So it was upon the next day and the next. And upon the fourth day she took an apple from another tree, and the peel broke beneath her knife, and she picked a second apple, and the peel fell in this shape or that; whereupon she went quickly back to her own tree. And always an apple fell into her lap, and always it told her that it was Silvio whom she loved.

There came a day when there was only one apple upon the tree. Then was she afraid, for she said, "How shall I know whom I love when the tree is empty?" So she went near to it. Very close, then, she felt to Silvio, and he to her; and suddenly she stretched out her arms, and said, "Apple tree, apple tree, you have seen whom it is that I love. Send him back to me!" And she put her arms round the tree and clung to it, crying, "Comfort me!" And it moved within her arms. Whereupon she was frightened and drew her arms away, putting her hands before her eyes . . . and when she opened her eyes, there was Silvio waiting for her, a golden apple in his hand. But there was no apple tree.

Then Silvio said to the Princess, "Whom is it that you love?" And she said, "Silvio." So they kissed each other. And the King, seeing them from his window, said, "Let him marry her, for he is a greater man than I." So they were married, and lived happily ever afterward, walking in the garden together, hand in hand.

And as soon as the story was finished, the sisters cried, "Read another and another." And so the eldest sister did.

Sparrow Tree
Square

WE will take the lady in green first. Her name is Diana Fitzpatrick Mauleverer James. She is the only child of Mr. and Mrs. Fitzpatrick Mauleverer James, who live at Number 27. Mrs. F. M. James wanted a boy, so that he could support them in their old age; but Mr. F. M. James said loftily: "No F. M. James, my dear, was ever any good at supporting. Where the F. M. Jameses shine is at

being supported. Let it be a girl, and let her marry some very rich man when she grows up. It shall be *his* proud privilege to tend the last of the F. M. Jameses in their middle age." So it was a girl.

Mrs. F. M. James was very fond of Diana, but she was fond of Mr. F. M. James, too, and a time came when she found that she couldn't look after both of them; for it would happen sometimes that, when Diana wanted to play trains, Mr. F. M. James didn't, or that when Mr. F. M. James did, then Diana had thought of some other game. So one day Mrs. F. M. James said:

"I think, dear, we had better get Diana a nurse, and then I can devote myself entirely to you."

"Certainly, my love, you should devote yourself entirely to me," said Mr. F. M. James, "but I cannot allow a common nurse to look after Diana Fitzpatrick Mauleverer. The F. M. Jameses have their pride."

"Then who is to look after her?" asked Diana's mother.

"She must look after herself."

So from that day Diana looked after herself. She woke herself in the morning, dressed herself, took

herself out for a walk, told herself to get-on-with-her-dinner-there-was-a-darling, sang herself to sleep in the afternoon, gave herself tea, brushed her hair and took herself downstairs to her father and mother, took herself back again if they were out, gave herself a bath, read to herself while she had her supper, and at the end of the day said good-night to herself and let herself in bed. When she was there, she made up little rhymes for herself, before going to sleep. One of them went like this:

Diana Fitzpatrick Mauleverer James
Was lucky to have the most beautiful names.
How awful for Fathers and Mothers to call
Their children Jemima! — or nothing at all!
But hers *were much wiser and kinder and cleverer,*
They called her Diana Fitzpatrick Mauleverer James.

I am telling you all this because I want you to understand how proud she felt on that first morning when she took herself to Sparrow Tree Square to feed the birds. There were other children there, but they had nurses with them. Sometimes the children ran away and pretended they didn't belong to the nurses,

and sometimes the nurses lagged behind and pretended they didn't belong to the children, but Diana Fitzpatrick Mauleverer James knew! She was the only entirely-all-by-herself person there. And she had given herself a bag of breadcrusts to feed the sparrows with, and she had let herself wear the green coat with fur trimmings, and she was utterly and entirely happy. She nodded to William and Wilhelmina Good, who were walking up and down in a very correct way, William in green, too, and Wilhelmina, who had been growing rather quickly lately, in blue. She laughed like anything at a little boy who was trying to count the sparrows and kept making it thirty instead of thirty-one, because one of them hid between his legs. How angry he was because he couldn't make it thirty-one! Silly little boy! She bowed politely to the Vanderdecken girls — over-dressed as usual — and agreed with them that it was a fine morning. They were feeding the sparrows, too, but they just had little bits of bread which their nurses gave them out of their pockets. Not like Diana, who had her crusts in a real grown-up bag!

14

Now then!

The sparrows flew round Diana Fitzpatrick Mauleverer James and sat waiting for her.

"All right, darlings," she said as she opened her bag.

Oh, dear! Oh, dear! Oh, dear!

She had forgotten to put the breadcrusts in!

The Twins

THEY are twins, and their names are William and Wilhelmina Good. When Mr. Good was told about them, he lit a cigar and said, "I shall call the boy William — after myself"; and then he thought for a long time and said, "And I shall call the girl Wilhelmina — after her brother." He threw his cigar away and went and told Mrs. Good, who had wanted to call them John and Jane. Mrs. Good said, "Very well, dear, but I don't like the name of William, and I shall call my dear little boy Billy for short." And Mr. Good said, "Certainly, my love, but if it comes to that,

I don't much care about the name of Wilhelmina, not for shouting up the stairs with, so my dear little girl had better be called Billy, too." Mrs. Good said, "Very well, dear, but won't it be rather confusing?" And Mr. Good said, "No, dear, not to people of any intelligence"; and he took out his watch at the end of its chain and swung it round and round and looked at it and said, "My watch is a fortnight fast," and put it back in his pocket and returned to his library.

The twins grew up, and they were so like each other that nobody knew which was which. Of course they ought to have had their names on their vests — *William Good, Wilhelmina Good* — but Nurse made a mistake about this. She bought the tape and marking ink, and she wrote the names, and she stitched them on; and, when all the vests were marked, she showed them proudly to Mrs. Good. And then it was discovered that by an accident she had marked them all *Billy Good*. When Mr. Good was told about this, he lit a cigar, and said, "Have people no intelligence at all? Next year, when they have grown out of these vests, I will mark the new ones myself." So next year he marked them all, in very neat printing, *W. Good.*

Luckily by this time Wilhelmina's hair had begun to curl. Every night Nurse spent ten minutes with a wet comb, combing it round her finger. William's hair curled naturally, too, but not so naturally as this, and in a little while you could tell at once which was Wilhelmina and which wasn't. If you will look at the picture, you will see how right I am about this. Mr. Good always says that he and I are the only people of any *real* intelligence left in the world . . . and that I am not what I was. However, I do my best; and I know I am right about this. The one with the curly hair is Wilhelmina.

One night when they were fast-asleep-like-good-children, Wilhelmina said:

"I'm very clever, I can hear in the dark I'm so clever."

"I'm as clever as anything," said William. "I'm too clever."

"I can hear snails breathing," said Wilhelmina.

"I can hear snails not breathing," said William.

Wilhelmina thought again.

"I can hear somebody out of the window calling Billy," she said.

"I told him to do it," said William.

"I'm going to see what he wants," said Wilhelmina. . . .

"Yes, I am," said Wilhelmina. . . .

"Shall I?" said Wilhelmina. . . .

"I think he meant *you*," said Wilhelmina.

"He meant you," said William. "He says it in a
different sort of voice when he means me."

"You're afraid to go," said Wilhelmina.

"I'm not afraid, but he gets very angry when the
wrong person goes," said William.

"He has a long red cap with a tassel on it," said
Wilhelmina.

"He has a long beard and green stockings," said
William.

"I'm going to see him," said Wilhelmina firmly.

"So am I going to see him."

"I'll go if you'll go."

"I'll go if you'll go."

"Let's both go."

"Yes, let's both go."

Very unwillingly they got out of bed, and stood,
hand in hand, on the nursery floor.

"I can't hear him now," said Wilhelmina hopefully.

"Nor can I hear him," said William at once.

"Yes, I can," said Wilhelmina unexpectedly, "because I'm so clever I hear so well."

"So can I," said William quickly.

They moved a little closer to the window.

"Does he get *very* angry if it's the wrong person?" asked Wilhelmina.

"He doesn't know, because his face is turned the wrong way round, so he's never quite sure."

"I knew his face was the wrong way round," said Wilhelmina hurriedly, "but I thought perhaps he had an Ooglie man with him to tell him."

William wondered anxiously what an Ooglie man was. So did Wilhelmina.

"No," said William. "He hasn't. Not this one."

"I'm not afraid," said both together. Tremblingly they pushed open the window, and leant out. . . .

SAIDA

Miss Waterlow
in Bed

THIS is Miss Waterlow in bed.

Mrs. Waterlow kissing her baby goodnight and saying:

"God bless you and keep you, my darling darlingest, my sweetheart, my little baby one."

Miss Waterlow gives a little faraway smile. She is thinking:

"I know a funny thing to think when I'm alone."

Mrs. Waterlow is looking at her as if she could never stop looking and saying:

"Thank you, and thank you, God, for giving me

my darling darlingest. You do understand, don't you, that it doesn't matter what happens to *me*, but oh! Don't let anything terrible happen to *her*!

Miss Waterlow is thinking:

"I shall pretend I'm big as the moon, and nobody can catch me I'm so big. Isn't that funny?"

"Good-night, beloved. Sleep well, my darling darlingest."

Miss Waterlow is remembering something . . . something very beautiful . . . but it all happened so long ago that she has forgotten the beginning of it before she remembers the end.

"Oh, my lovely, when you look like that you make me want to cry. What are you thinking of, darlingest?"

Miss Waterlow won't tell.

Yet perhaps for a moment Mrs. Waterlow has been there, too.

"God bless you, my lovely," she says, and puts out the light.

Miss Waterlow is alone.

Miss Waterlow at this time was one. It is a tremendous age to be, and often she would lie on her

back and laugh to think of all the babies who were none. When she was six months old, Mr. Waterlow, who was a poet, wrote some verses about her and he slipped them proudly into Mrs. Waterlow's hand one evening. Owing to a misunderstanding, they were used to wedge the nursery window, which rattled at night; and though they wedged very delightfully for some time, Mr. Waterlow couldn't help feeling a little disappointed. Mrs. Waterlow was, of course, as sorry as she could be when she understood what had happened, but it was then too late. As Mr. Waterlow said: Once you have bent a piece of poetry, it is never quite the same again. Fortunately for all of us, two lines at the end, torn off so as to make the wedge the right thickness, have survived. They go like this:

She never walks, and she never speaks —
And we've had her for weeks *and* weeks *and* weeks!"

Now the truth was that Miss Waterlow could speak if she wanted to, but she had decided to wait until she was quarter past one. The reason was that she had such lovely things to remember, *if only she could remember them.* You can't talk *and* think. For a year and

25

a quarter she would just lie on her back and remember . . . and then when she had it all quite clear in her mind, she would tell them all about it. But nobody can speak without practice. So every night, as soon as she was alone, she practiced.

She practiced now.

"Teddy!" she called.

Down on the floor, at the foot of her bed, Teddy-bear, whose head was nodding on his chest, woke up with a start.

"What is it?" he grumbled.

"Are you asleep, Teddy?"

"I *are* and I *aren't*," said Teddy.

"I *thought* I *were*, and I *weren't*," said Miss Waterlow.

"Well, well, what is it?"

"What's a word for a lovely — a lovely — *you* know what I mean — and all of a sudden — only you don't because — what *is* the word, Teddy?"

"Condensed milk," said Teddy.

"I don't *fink* it is," said Miss Waterlow.

"As near as you can get nowadays."

Miss Waterlow sighed. She never seemed to get very near.

"Perhaps I shall never tell them," said Miss Waterlow sadly. "Perhaps they don't have the word."

"Perhaps they don't," said Teddy. "It's a funny thing about them," he went on, waking up slightly, "what a few words they *have* got. Take 'condensed milk' as an example. It does, but it isn't *really*, if you see what I mean. That's why I never talk to 'em now. They don't get any *richness* into their words — they don't get any what I call flavor. There's no *bite.*"

"I want a word —"

"Better go to sleep," said Teddy, his head nodding suddenly again.

"Shan't I ever be able to tell them?" asked Miss Waterlow wistfully.

"Never," said Teddy sleepily. "They've got the wrong words."

Miss Waterlow lay there, wrapt in drowsy and enchanted memories of that golden land to which she could never quite return. She would tell them all about it some day . . . but not now . . . not now . . . not now. . . .

She gave a little sigh and was asleep.

Poor Anne

SHE was christened Anne Lavender, so that her full name was Anne Lavender Lavender. This was an idea of Mr. Lavender's. He was very proud of his family, and it distressed him to think that when his daugher, the beautiful Miss Lavender, married, her name might be something quite ugly, like Winks.

"Whereas," he explained to Anne's mamma, "if we call her Anne Lavender Lavender, her name, when

she marries this man Winks, will be Anne Lavender-Winks, and people will know at once that she is one of us."

"They will know that anyhow," said Mrs. Lavender, bending over her baby. "She is just like her old Daddy, aren't you, darling?"

Anne, being then about none, did not reply.

"She has my hair, certainly," said Mr. Lavender, and he stroked his raven locks proudly.

He was very dark, and Mrs. Lavender was very fair, and they had often wondered which of them Anne would be like. He used to say, "I do hope she will be like *you*, darling," and she would say, "I would rather she were like *you*, dearest," and he would say, "Well, well, we shall see." And now she was dark. She was dark, like him; and she was called Anne Lavender Lavender, which was his own idea; and he felt very happy about it all.

And then one day a surprising thing happened. All her dark hair fell off, and she became as fair as fair — just like her mamma.

"What a pity!" said Mrs. Lavender. "I did want her to be like you."

"She's much prettier like you," said Mr. Lavender gallantly, though secretly he was a little hurt.

But he soon got over it. By the time Anne was one and a bit, he had decided that the only color for very small fat girls was fair. He used to gaze at her sometimes, and say to himself, "I shan't let her marry that fellow Winks now, she's much too good for him. She's lovely — and just like her mother."

And then another very surprising thing happened. Her hair suddenly became red. Not golden-red or chestnut-red, but really-carrotty-red. Red! And nobody in Mr. Lavender's family or Mrs. Lavender's family had ever had red hair before!

It was then that one or two people began calling her Poor Anne. They didn't all do it at first — just one or two of them. "What a pity about Poor Anne," they said. "She used to have such lovely flaxen hair." And when they were talking about Christmas presents, they used to say, "And, of course, there's Poor Anne; we mustn't forget *her*."

Mr. Lavender was terribly upset about it all. He wrote to the editors of several papers, and asked them to say whether, if a child's hair had once *not*

31

been red, and then *was* red, whether it would ever *not* be red again, if it once *hadn't* been. Some of them didn't answer, and some said that Time Would Show, and two of them said that Red Hair Was Very Becoming. But, of course, that wasn't what Mr. Lavender wanted to know.

Mrs. Lavender didn't mind so much. She had just decided to have another baby called David Lavender.

David was fair. Fairer than Anne had ever been, fairer than his mother had ever been. All his aunts came and looked at him, and they said to each other, "Isn't his hair lovely?" And then they *all* said to each other, "What a pity about Poor Anne!"

Poor Anne didn't mind. She was much too happy taking care of her little brother. You see, she knew why her own hair had gone red. It was because she had caught that terrible cold when she was two, through getting her feet wet. So it was *most important* that David should never, never catch cold, because a girl with carrotty hair was just Poor Anne, but a boy with carrotty hair was Oh-*poor*-David. And her father would be so miserable that he wouldn't ever write to the papers again, and it would be all her fault.

So she did all she possibly could to keep David's hair the right color, and she did it so well that one day Mr. Lavender said:

"Poor Anne. She won't be beautiful, but she'll be very useful, and I think I shall let her marry the Winks fellow after all."

And then he murmured to himself, "Anne Lavender-Winks. How *right* I was about that!"

A Voyage to India

RAINING, still raining! Oh, dear, oh, dear! But what, you say to yourself, is a little rain? Jane Ann must be patient. She must stay at home and play with her delightful toys this afternoon, and then perhaps tomorrow morning the sun will come out, and she will be able to run about in the fields again. After all, it isn't every little girl who has a rabbit, and a horse and cart, and an india-rubber ball to play with. Come, come, Jane Ann!

How little you understand!

Today was the day. Tomorrow will be too late. Perhaps even now if it cleared up — but each time that she has said this, down has come another cloud. She tried shutting her eyes; she did try that. She tried shutting here eyes and saying, "One, two, three, four — I'll count twenty and then I'll open them, and please, will you let the rain stop by then, please, because it's too terribly important, you know why." Yes, she counted twenty; quickly up to twelve, and then more slowly to fifteen, and then sixteen . . . seventeen . . . eighteen . . . nineteen . . . and then, so slowly that it wasn't really fair, but she wanted to make it easier for God, twe . . . twe . . . twe . . . TWENTY! But it went on raining. She tried holding her breath; she said that if she held her breath a very long time, longer than anyone in the whole world had ever held it before, then when she stopped holding it, it would stop raining. Wouldn't it? But it didn't. So she stood at the window and watched the raindrops sliding down the pane; and she said — and she *knew* this would do it — that if *this* raindrop got to the bottom of the pane before the other, then it

would stop raining, but that if the other one did, then it wouldn't stop . . . and when they were halfway down, she said, No, it was the other way about, and if this one got there *last*, then . . . But still it went on raining.

You see, it was the day she was going to India. Her father and mother lived in India, and she remembered them quite well. She was to live with Aunt Mary until they came home, which was next year, and sometimes she got tired of waiting.

"Couldn't they come tomorrow?" she asked.

"Not tomorrow," said Aunt Mary, "because they are very busy, but it won't be long now."

Then Jane Ann had her lovely idea. If they were too busy to come to her, she would go to them.

She counted up all her money and thought it would be just enough, if she walked all the way. And every day that week, when she went out with her nurse, she bought something nourishing, like buns or chocolates, and put them in her special box. And every evening she looked inside the box, and then shut her eyes and thought very hard of her father and mother and didn't eat any of it. And when the box

was full, it was Friday night, and tomorrow was the day.

She said good-bye to Rabbit that night. They all wanted to come, but Rabbit most. Rabbit had a special pink ribbon round his neck to come by, and he had never been to India before, so he was terribly excited. But Jane Ann said, No, he couldn't, because India was full of fierce tigers, and tigers ate rabbits. Rabbit saw that it wouldn't do to be eaten by a tiger, but he thought he could dodge them. He was very disappointed when Jane Ann told him that even dodgy rabbits got eaten by tigers in India. "Even *very* dodgy rabbits?" he asked wistfully. "Yes," said Jane Ann, "even *very* dodgy rabbits." But she felt so sorry for him when she said this that she took off his pink ribbon and hid it away in a drawer, in case she felt she *couldn't* leave him behind in the morning.

They were all to see her off. She arranged them in the window — Horse and Cart, House, Ball and Rabbit — so that she would be able to wave to them for quite a long way. Of course, after you had gone a long way you had to turn to the right, and then you wouldn't see them anymore. That was when she

would first open her box, because she would be feeling so lonely. It was wonderful how unlonely chocolate made you.

Looking out of the window next morning, Rabbit saw that it was raining.

"Perhaps she won't go now," he said, and he was very excited.

After breakfast Jane Ann looked out of the window, too.

"It will stop soon," she said cheerfully.

And she stood there waiting for it to stop. . . .

Barbara's
Birthday

THEY are being photographed. Names, reading
from left to right:

Susan, Henry Dog, Barbara, Mrs. Perkins, Helen.

Of course, they are not really being photographed,
but Helen said, "Let's pretend that we are, and that
it's going to be in the papers tomorrow." So she put
one hand on Mrs. Perkins, to show how fond she was
of the cat, and took the other one off the table, to
show how well-brought-up she was, and said "Go!"

Well, you see what happened. Susan and Barbara
weren't ready for it. They were both eating, and both
had their elbows on the table. It would be a terrible

thing if the photograph came out in the paper like that. Couldn't the man take another one?

Helen said, No, it was the last one he had. He had been taking photographs all the day of "Scenes in the Village on the Occasion of Miss Barbara's Sixth Birthday" and he only had two left when he came to the house. One was "A Corner of the Stables Taken From the North Side of the Lake," and the other was "Miss Barbara Entertains a Few Friends to Tea, reading from left to right."

Barbara said, "Oh!"

Susan said, "Well, I don't mind, because it's not my birthday."

Helen said, "It was the man's fault for taking all those ones in the village."

Susan said, "My birthday's on April the Fifteenth and I'm five, and Henry's three and his birthday's the same day as mine, isn't that funny?"

And Barbara said, "Well, I know I'm six."

Then they all began to eat again.

But if Barbara was six, where was the big birthday cake with six candles on it? Ah!

You see, Barbara lived in a big town, and the Doctor

looked at her one day and said "H'm!" Then he asked her to put out her tongue, and when he saw it, he said, "Tut-tut-tut!" Then he put his fingers on her wrist and looked at his watch but it wasn't working, and he said, "Come, come, this won't do." And just when Barbara was going to say, "Would you like to try *my* watch?" the Doctor turned to Barbara's father and mother and said, "She wants a change." So it was decided that on Monday Barbara should take her nurse into the country for a change.

"But what about my birthday?" said Barbara. "Will I be at home for my birthday?"

Barbara's father brought out his pocket diary, and it was found that she couldn't get home again until two days after her birthday.

"Never mind," said her mother; "You can have your birthday three days later this year."

"And a very extra special one to make up," said her father.

So that was that, and Barbara didn't really mind a bit, because she loved being in the country, and she had her birthday to look forward to when she got home again.

Now there was a family living in the village called — I forget the name, and the family was Mr. and Mrs. Somebody, Helen Somebody, Susan Somebody, Henry Dog and Mrs. Perkins. Barbara got very friendly with them, and one day Helen and Susan were coming to tea with her, because it was her last day but one.

"I wish you could stay to April the Fifteenth," said Susan, "because it's my birthday and I'm five, and Henry's three, isn't it funny?"

"I'm six as soon as I get back," said Barbara. "I would have been six today, if I had been well."

"Do you mean it's your birthday?" said Helen excitedly.

Barbara explained how, because of having a change, she wasn't being six till three days later this year.

"But you *are* six, you *are* six," said Helen, jumping up and down. "Isn't she, Susan?"

Susan said: "I'm five on April the —"

"Of *course* you're six, so we must make it a birthday party. And please will you invite Mr. Henry Dog and

Mrs. Perkins as well as us, so as to make it a big party?"

Barbara promised; and when her guests arrived, Helen had brought some flowers to make the party look more exciting. She had also made up a rhyme to say; at least, she and her father had made it up between them, and Helen said it.

> Barbara is six today
> Hooray, hooray, hooray, hooray!

Then they all had tea.

And Helen and Susan and Henry Dog and Mrs. Perkins thought it was a lovely tea. But all the time Barbara was saying to herself, "Only three more days, and then I shall have my *real* birthday."

The Magic Hill

O NCE upon a time there was a King who had seven children. The first three were boys, and he was glad about this because a King likes to have three sons; but when the next three were sons also, he was not so glad, and he wished that one of them had been a daughter. So the Queen said, "The next shall be a daughter." And it was, and they decided to call her Daffodil.

When the Princess Daffodil was a month old, the King and Queen gave her a great party in the Palace for the christening, and the Fairy Mumruffin was invited to be Godmother to the little Princess.

"She is a good fairy," said the King to the Queen, "and I hope she will give our Daffodil something that will be useful to her. Beauty or Wisdom or Riches or — "

"Or Goodness," said the Queen.

"Or Goodness, as I was about to remark," said the King.

So you will understand how anxious they were when Fairy Mumruffin looked down at the sleeping Princess in her cradle and waved her wand.

"They have called you Daffodil," she said, and then she waved her wand again:

> *Let Daffodil*
> *The gardens fill.*
> *Wherever you go*
> *Flowers shall grow.*

There was a moment's silence while the King tried to think this out.

"What was that?" he whispered to the Queen. "I didn't quite get that."

"Wherever she walks flowers are going to grow," said the Queen. "I think it's sweet."

"Oh," said the King. "Was that all? She didn't say anything about —"

"No."

"Oh, well."

He turned to thank the Fairy Mumruffin, but she had already flown away.

It was nearly a year later that the Princess first began to walk, and by this time everybody had forgotten about the Fairy's promise. So the King was rather surprised, when he came back from hunting one day, to find that his favorite courtyard, where he used to walk when he was thinking, was covered with flowers.

"What does this mean?" he said sternly to the chief gardener.

"I don't know, Your Majesty," said the gardener, scratching his head. "It isn't *my* doing."

"Then who has done it? Who has been here today?"

"Nobody, Your Majesty, except her Royal Highness, Princess Daffodil, as I've been told, though how she found her way there, such a baby and all, bless her sweet little —"

"That will do," said the King. "You may go."

For now he remembered. This was what the Fairy Mumruffin had promised.

That evening the King and the Queen talked the matter over very seriously before they went to bed.

"It is quite clear," said the King, "that we cannot let Daffodil run about everywhere. That would never do. She must take her walks on the beds. She must be carried across the paths. It will be annoying in a way, but in a way it will be useful. We shall be able to do without most of the gardeners."

"Yes, dear," said the Queen.

So Daffodil as she grew up was only allowed to walk on the beds, and the other children were very jealous of her because they were only allowed to walk on the paths; and they thought what fun it would be if only they were allowed to run about on the beds just once. But Daffodil thought what fun it would be if she could run about the paths like other boys and girls.

One day, when she was about five years old, a Court Doctor came to see her. And when he looked at her tongue, he said to the Queen:

"Her Royal Highness needs more exercise. She must run about more. She must climb hills and roll down them. She must hop and skip and jump. In short, Your Majesty, although she is a Princess she must do what other little girls do."

"Unfortunately," said the Queen, "she is not like other little girls." And she sighed and looked out of the window. And out of the window, at the far end of the garden, she saw a little green hill where no flowers grew. So she turned back to the Court Doctor and said, "You are right; she must be as other little girls."

So she went to the King, and the King gave the Princess Daffodil the little green hill for her very own. And every day the Princess Daffodil played there, and flowers grew; and every evening the girls and boys of the countryside came and picked the flowers.

So they called it the Magic Hill. And from that day onward flowers have always grown on the Magic Hill, and boys and girls have laughed and played and picked them.

The
Baby Show

MR. THEOPILUS BANKS was a very important man. His friends called him Theo. I forget what he did exactly, but it was very important, and if he didn't do it, then where should we all be? I don't know. Everything depended on Mr. Banks.

He had three children. The first was a girl, and she was called Jessica Banks after her mother. The next was a boy, and he was called Theophilus Banks, after his father, Theophilus Banks. Some people thought it would be rather confusing having two Theophiluses Bankses in the family, but Mr. Banks thought not. He said that for many years the child would be Master Banks, and if they liked they could call him Phil for short; and that by the time he was old enough to be Mr. Banks, his father would be Judge Banks or Professor Banks, or Colonel Banks or President Banks — he hadn't quite decided yet. So the baby was called Phil for short. And then, later on, there was a third child, and as Mr. Banks couldn't very well call him Theophilus, too, he decided to keep as much of the name in the family as was possible. So the Baby was called Theodore, or Toddy for short.

Mr. Banks played golf. He was a very active man, and he played more golf in an afternoon than anybody else at his club. Sometimes the friends he was playing with would stop for tea after hitting the ball only seventy-five times, but Mr. Banks would never stop until he had hit it a hundred and twenty times. He was that sort of man. You would have thought that they would have given him a prize for being so active, but they didn't. They always gave it to the others. Almost everybody in the club was given a little silver cup except Mr. Banks. He used to feel very unhappy about it. Whenever he and Mrs. Banks went out to dinner with their friends, they would always see a silver cup on the table, and Mr. Binks (if that was the name of the friend) would explain to Mr. Banks how he had won the cup last Saturday, and Mrs. Binks would explain to Mrs. Banks how her husband had won it. And Mr. and Mrs. Banks would go home feeling very disheartened about it.

One day Mrs. Banks read in the paper that there was going to be a Baby Show in the town. She told Jessica, and Jessica said at once. "Oh, let's put Toddy in! What fun!"

"Put Toddy in, put Toddy in," cried Phil, thinking it was some sort of pond, and how funny Toddy would look in it.

"Oh, do let's," said Jessica, "and then if he won, Father would have a silver cup like the others."

Mrs. Banks suddenly remembered that it was Father's birthday next week. He had everything he wanted except a silver cup. How happy he would be if he could win one just in time for his birthday!

So Master Theodore Banks was entered for the Baby Show. Of course it was to be a secret from Mr. Banks, so every day when he was at the office where everything depended on him, the others used to get together and wonder how they could improve Toddy, so as to make sure that he would win the prize.

Mrs. Banks thought he was perfect as he was.

Jessica thought that he would have been perfect if his hair had been a little more curly.

Phil thought that if he was put in a pond and made to swim, he would be much stronger. *And* perfecter.

So Jessica brushed and brushed and brushed his hair every day; and every day Phil tried to get hold of him so as to strengthen him. But Mrs. Banks kept him on the chest of drawers, so that Jessica could brush his hair and Phil couldn't quite reach him, and she thought to herself, "I believe he *will* win the prize after all." And every day when Mr. Banks came home from golf, she looked at him to see if he had won a silver cup; but he hadn't.

Mr. Banks hadn't been thinking much about his birthday. He knew he was 35 or 107 or something, and he knew it was this week, but nobody was more surprised than he when he came down to breakfast on Thursday, and found a beautiful parcel on his plate. You can guess how excited he was.

"Well, well, well, what can this be?" he said, and Phil nudged Jessica, and Jessica smiled at her mother and Phil jumped about and said, "Open it! Open it!" So Mr. Banks opened it.

"Well, well, well!" he said.

It was a silver cup.

"But what — ?" he said.

Then he turned it round, and on the other side he saw:

FIRST PRIZE
(Division I)
WON BY
THEO BANKS

"But who —?" he said.

Then they explained how Theodore had won the prize, and how there hadn't been room to get *all* his name in, so they had had to put Theo.

"Well, well, well," said Mr. Theo. Banks again.

So, from that day, whenever Mr. and Mrs. Binks came to dinner, there was the silver cup on the table!

"Now we shall all live happy ever after, shan't we?" said Jessica to her mother.

And they did.

The Three Daughters of M. Dupont

WHEN Monsieur Dupont was a Frenchman, he had three daughters, and their names were Anne-Marie, Thérèse and *la p'tite* Georgette. But when he became an American, for a change, he called himself Mr. Dewpond, and his daughters were called Anne Mary, Terry and George.

Mrs. Dewpond (who still called herself Madame Dupont when nobody was looking) had a linen-cupboard of which she was very proud, and it was her one delight to keep it always full of the most beautiful linen. Linen fascinated her, just as kittens fascinate other people, and money fascinates my Uncle James. She was never tired of buying it, and running her fingers over it, and holding it against her cheek, and then tucking it lovingly away in her cupboard; and whenever she had a birthday, her three daughters would put all their savings together and buy her a tablecloth or a pair of dusters, so that Mrs. Dewpond should say, "My darlings, but how they are ravishing!" They loved to hear her say this.

One day Mrs. Dewpond was not very well; and then there were more days when she was no better; and first a doctor came, and then a nurse came, and then she and the nurse went away into the country together to see if that would do her any good. And all the time Mr. Dewpond went about the house saying "T'chk, t'chk, t'chk" to himself, and looking very miserable; and Anne Mary wrote to her mother every day to say that they were all getting on all right and did want her back so badly; and Terry ended up her prayers every night with, "And may she suddenly come back tomorrow morning about half past seven, so that I can wake up and there she is"; and George kissed the door of her Mother's empty bedroom every time she passed it, as a sort of friendly habit; and all the house called to her to come back to it.

And at last there came a day when Mr. Dewpond had a letter saying that Mrs. Dewpond was very nearly well again and would be home again on Saturday afternoon. This was on the Monday, so they had less than a week to wait, and they were all just as happy as they could be, thinking of it.

"We must celebrate it," said Terry solemnly.

George didn't know what "celebrate" meant, so Anne Mary explained it to her until she did know, and then they all wondered how they should do it.

"I know," said Terry suddenly. "Let's send all the linen to the wash, and then it will be lovely and clean and smelling lavendery when she comes back to it."

Anne Mary was not sure if this was a good thing to do. There was such a lot of it, and it would look so funny on the bill if they suddenly had a hundred and twelve table-cloths, and only one white shirt, and —

"Well, anyhow, George thinks it's a lovely idea," said Terry carelessly, "and you know what fun it will be putting it all back again."

The thought of putting it all back again was too much for Anne Mary.

"Very well, darlings," she said, "we'll do it. Come along."

So they counted it out. There were 112 tablecloths, 42 bath towels, 73 small towels, 26 pairs of sheets, 229 pillowcases, and more dusters than I can possibly put down here. And they all went to the laundry together. On the Saturday morning they all came back (except one duster) and Anne Mary, Terry, and George put them in the cupboard as neat as neat, George being particularly helpful. And then they waited for their mother.

She came at last. Anne Mary said that she was prettier than ever, and Mr. Dewpond said she had never looked so well, and Terry and George thought that she was even nicer to kiss than she had ever been before. For some time they all talked together about everything, and you could see that Mrs. Dewpond couldn't help thinking of her linen-cupboard now and then, but she didn't say anything; and Terry and George kept whispering to each other, "Won't she be surprised when she sees?" — and sometimes George

said to Anne Mary, "How surprised do you think she'll be?" At last she got up, saying, "Well, I think I'll just —" and they knew where she was going, and they all went with her. She threw open the chest, and of course, she knew at once what had happened. She just clasped her hands and cried, "My darlings, but how they are ravishing!" And then they all four hugged each other.

Later on, when he saw the bill, Mr. Dewpond clasped his hands and cried, too.

Castles by the Sea

T HIS is a story about Belinda, and, as it is the last, I think I shall tell it to you in poetry. Belinda is the one in mauve, and I could have written much better poetry if she had been in brown or blue, but mothers never think of things like this when they dress their children. However, she has a little red on her cap, which may be useful. We shall see.

FIRST VERSE

Belinda Brown was six or so,
Belinda had a grown-up spade,
Belinda Brown was six, and oh!
The castle that Belinda made!

65

That's the first verse; and now, if anybody asks you what her name was, you can answer at once "Belinda, because it says so in one of the lines."

SECOND VERSE

Belinda Brown was six or so,
Although she looked a little more,
But she was only six, and oh!
The bonny cap Belinda wore!

Now you can tell everybody Belinda's age. Six. With a good poem like this one doesn't want to be in a hurry.

THIRD VERSE

Belinda's cap was mauve and red —
A pity that it wasn't blue —
But it was red and mauve instead,
And very pretty colors, too.

I think I shall go straight on to the next verse without saying anything about that one.

FOURTH VERSE
(This is going to be a good one)

Belinda had a bathing-gown
Which had been brown a week before;

The envy of her native town
The bathing-gown Belinda wore!

I like that verse. Besides being good poetry, it explains everything. You see, Belinda's Aunt Rotunda had given her the beautiful cap, and when Belinda went to dig castles in the sand, she decided to wear the cap to keep the sun off her head, but to wear the bathing-dress, too, so as not to mind if she got wet, which was her own idea and none of the other children had thought of it. So her mother said, "Then we'd better dye the dress mauve," to which her father replied, "Wouldn't it be easier to dye the cap brown?" And Belinda's mother said, "I think, dear, it might hurt Aunt Rotunda's feelings." So —

> *Belinda wore*
> *   Her bathing-gown*
> *   (A brilliant brown*
> *The week before).*
> *The local store*
> *   Had toned it down,*
> *   The bathing-gown*
> *Belinda wore.*

I think it looks nicer spread out like that. I will tell you a secret now. When people pay you to write poetry for them (as they often do), they pay you so much for every line you write, so sometimes you feel that a verse looks nice spread out, and sometimes the man who is paying you feels that it doesn't. It's just a matter of taste.

FIFTH VERSE
(I'm not counting the last one,
because it's a different shape from the others)

Belinda Brown was not afraid,
(Belinda was as brave as three)
And in the castle she had made
She waited for the rising sea.
Belinda was as brave as three,
Belinds was as brave as eight;
She waited calmly while the sea
Came in at a tremendous rate.

And now we are coming to the sad part of the story. There was Belinda, as you see her in the picture, not a bit afraid, and suddenly —

SIXTH VERSE

A monster wave came rolling on,
It washed Belinda's castle down,
And in a moment they were gone —
The castle and Belinda Brown.

But where was Belinda? That was what all the other children said. And when Mr. and Mrs. Brown came down to the beach they began saying it, too: "Where *is* Belinda?" Nobody knew. However, it was all right.

SEVENTH VERSE

They found her later on the hill
A mile or so above the town,
A little out of breath, but still
Undoubtedly Belinda Brown.

You can imagine how excited they all were. All but Belinda. They came rushing up to her, saying, "Oh, Belinda, are you hurt?" and, "Are you *sure* you're all right, Belinda darling?" And some of the more polite ones, who had never seen her before, said, "I trust that you have not injured yourself in any way, Miss Brown?" And what did Belinda say?

LAST VERSE

Belinda tossed a scornful head —
Belinda was as brave as brave —
Belinda laughed at them and said,
  "Oh, wasn't that a lovely *wave?"*

ABOUT THIS BOOK

A Gallery of Children was first published in June 1925, just after A. A. Milne's *When We Were Very Young* and it is the only Milne and le Mair collaboration. Until that time Milne had been known primarily for his adult plays and short stories.

After the success of *When We Were Very Young*, Milne's publishers were clamoring for him to write another children's book of his own. It was le Mair's agent, Mildred Massey, who first thought to bring le Mair's artwork to Milne.

When Milne first saw le Mair's *Our Old Nursery Rhymes* (1911), he wrote Massey.

> *I have just looked through the nursery rhyme book. The pictures are absolutely charming. If the new ones were as full of detail I could write pages about them. . . . And what's more I should be doing it.*

Henriette Willebeek le Mair was a contemporary of Kate Greenaway's and has been compared to Greenaway for her skill in capturing the very essence of childhood in her artwork. Ms. le Mair illustrated fourteen books in all, including *Our Old Nursery Rhymes* and *Little Songs of Long Ago*. Her artwork for *A Gallery of Children* was created in the early 1920s and appeared as illustrations in magazines such as *The Ladies' Home Journal* and *McCall's*. After her marriage she joined the Sufi movement and became more and more interested in Eastern culture. Le Mair signed the illustrations for *A Gallery of Children* with her Sufi name, Saida.

72